The Twelve Days of Christmas

The Twelve Days of
CHRISTMAS

Illustrated by Don Daily

RP|CLASSICS

PHILADELPHIA • LONDON

Books published by Running Press are available at special discounts for bulk purchases in
the United States by corporations, institutions, and other organizations. For more infor-
mation, please contact the Special Markets Department at the Perseus Books Group, 2300
Chestnut Street, Suite 200, Philadelphia, PA 19103, or call (800) 810-4145, ext. 5000, or
e-mail special.markets@perseusbooks.com.

ISBN 978-0-7624-0764-4
Library of Congress Control Number: 00-132365

E-book ISBN 978-0-7624-4312-3

15   14   13   12   11   10   9   8
Digit on the right indicates the number of this printing

Designed by Frances J. Soo Ping Chow
Edited by Greg Jones and Danielle McCole
Typography: Fairfield

Published by Running Press Kids Classics
An Imprint of Running Press Book Publishers
A Member of the Perseus Books Group
2300 Chestnut Street
Philadelphia, PA 19103–4371

Visit us on the web!
www.runningpress.com/kids

On the 1st day of Christmas
my true love gave to me

A partridge in a pear tree.

On the **2nd** day of Christmas
my true love gave to me

Two turtle doves and a partridge in a pear tree.

On the 3rd day of Christmas

my true love gave to me

Three French hens, two turtle doves, and a partridge in a pear tree.

On the 4th day of Christmas
my true love gave to me

Four calling birds, three French hens, two turtle doves,
and a partridge in a pear tree.

On the 5th day of Christmas
my true love gave to me

Five golden rings, four calling birds, three French hens, two turtle doves, and a partridge in a pear tree.

On the **6th** day of Christmas my true love gave to me

Six geese a-laying, five golden rings, four calling birds, three French hens, two turtle doves, and a partridge in a pear tree.

On the 7th day of Christmas

my true love gave to me

Seven swans a-swimming, six geese a-laying, five golden rings,
four calling birds, three French hens, two turtle doves, and
a partridge in a pear tree.

On the 8th day of Christmas
my true love gave to me